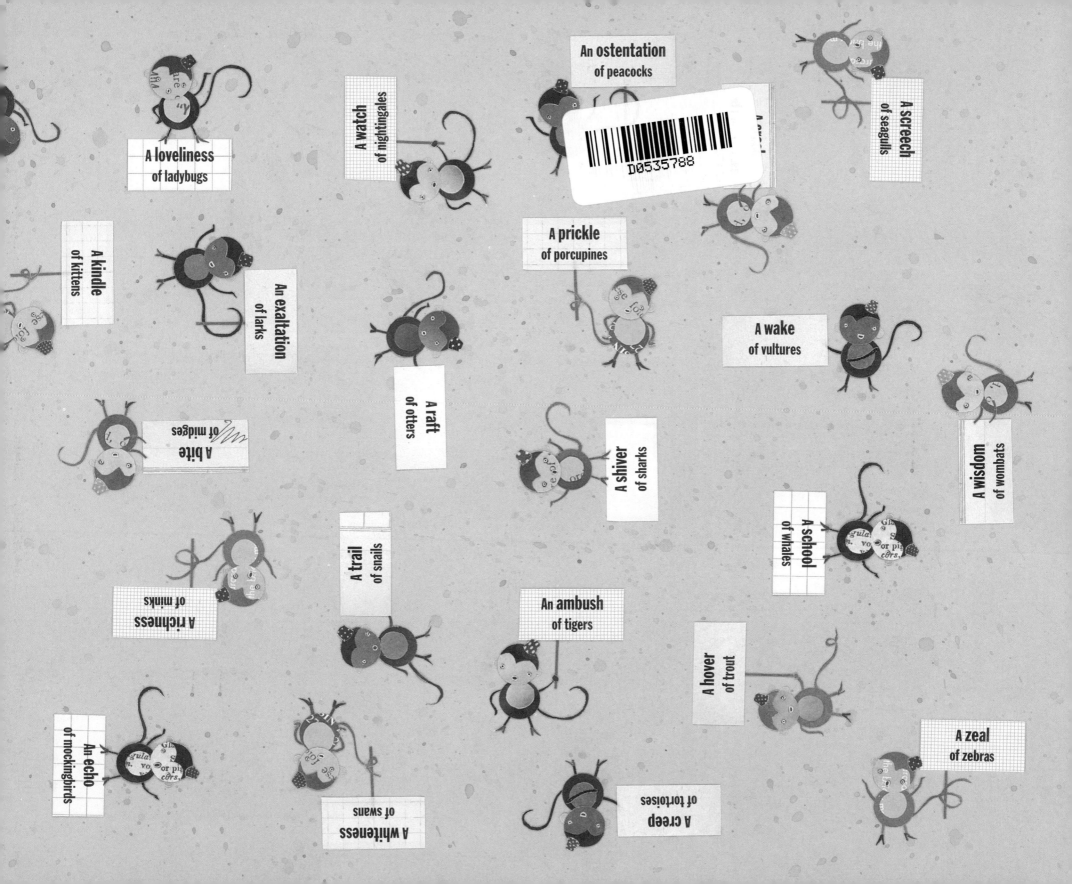

An ostentation
of peacocks

A watch
of nightingales

A screech
of seagulls

A loveliness
of ladybugs

A kindle
of kittens

An exaltation
of larks

A prickle
of porcupines

A wake
of vultures

A bite
of midges

A raft
of otters

A shiver
of sharks

A wisdom
of wombats

A richness
of minks

A trail
of snails

A school
of whales

An ambush
of tigers

A hover
of trout

An echo
of mockingbirds

A whiteness
of swans

A creep
of tortoises

A zeal
of zebras

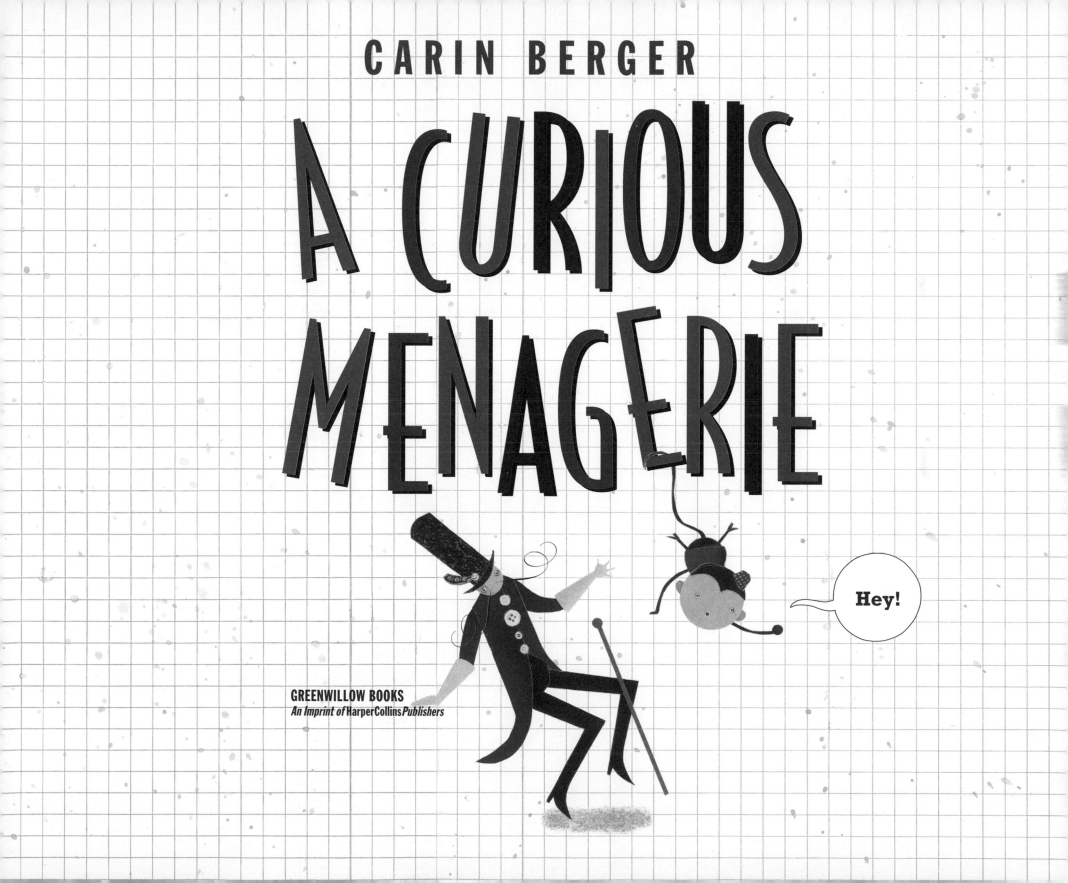

Collages were used to prepare the full-color art.

The text types are Franklin Gothic Extra Condensed and Rockwell Bold.

Library of Congress Cataloging-in-Publication Data

Names: Berger, Carin, author, illustrator.

Title: A curious menagerie / Carin Berger.

Description: First edition. | New York, NY : Greenwillow Books,

an imprint of HarperCollinsPublishers, [2019] |

Summary: "Introduces readers to sixty unusual and engaging collective nouns

ranging from a flamboyance of flamingos to a mischief of mice. Includes a note

about the origin of the collective nouns featured in the book"—Provided by publisher.

Identifiers: LCCN 2018033140 | ISBN 9780062644572 (hardback)

Subjects: | CYAC: Animals, Nomenclature—Fiction. |

English language—Collective nouns—Fiction.

Classification: LCC PZ7.B45134 Cur 2019 | DDC [E]—dc23

LC record available at https://lccn.loc.gov/2018033140

19 20 21 22 23 SCP 10 9 8 7 6 5 4 3 2 1

First Edition

Greenwillow Books

A group of giraffes is called a **TOWER** of giraffes.

So tall! And a group of penguins?

A
SCURRY
of
SQUIRRELS
→

Several squirrels
are called a
SCURRY.

A scurry of
squirrels!
Look at them go!
How about
a crowd
of crows?

RACCOONS

A gathering
of raccoons
is called a
GAZE
of raccoons.

Peekaboo!
What do you
call a mess
of mice?

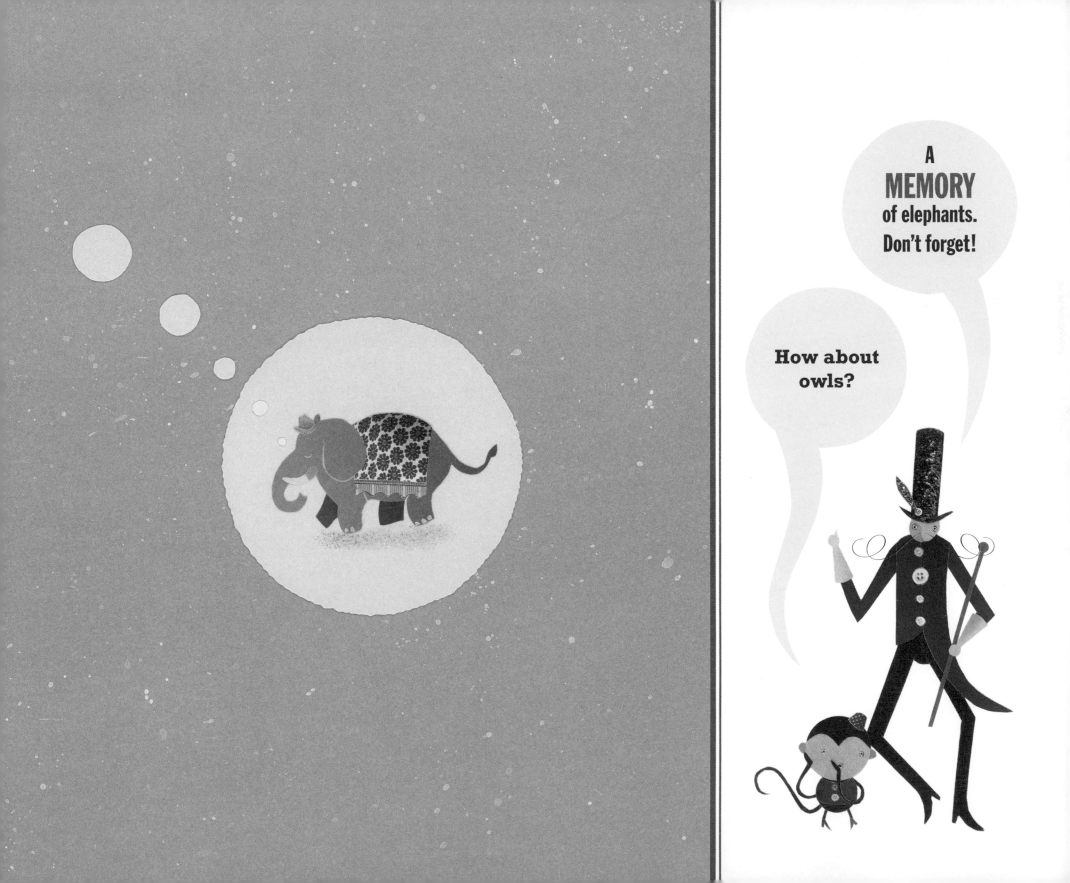

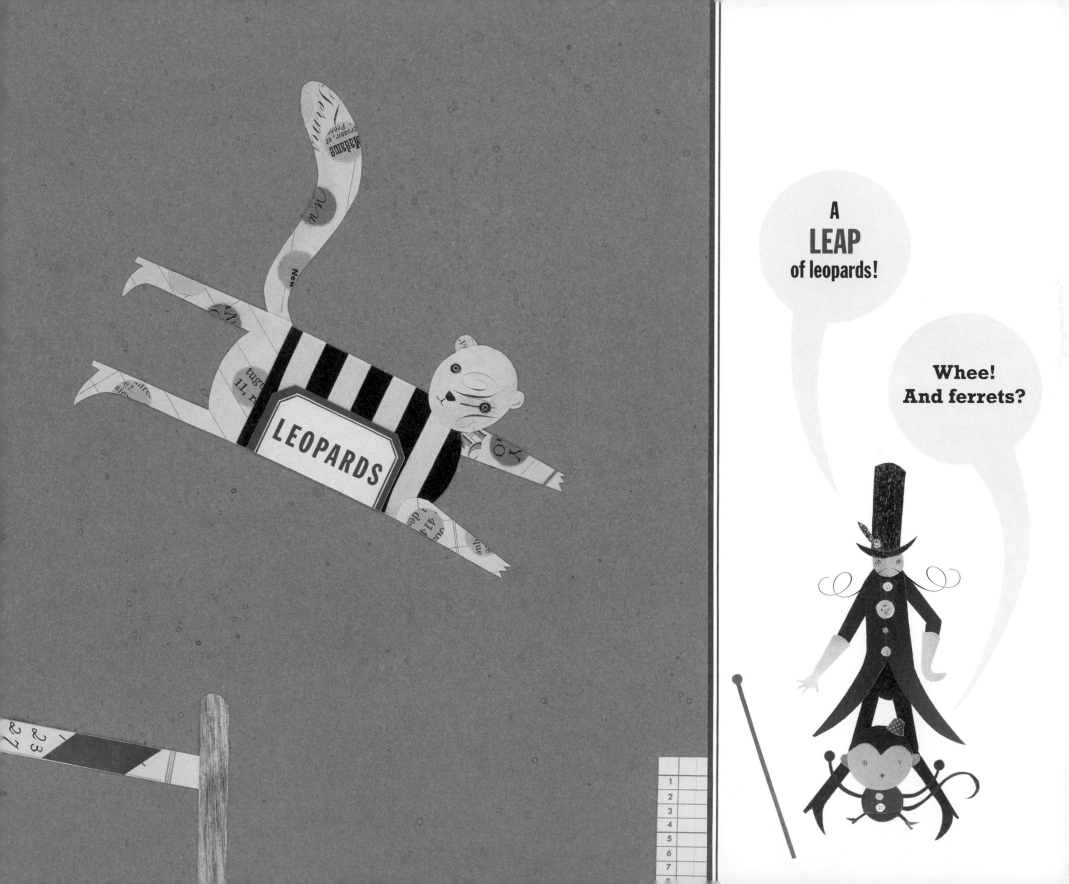

A bunch of ferrets
is called a
BUSINESS
of ferrets.

Hmmm. . . .
What do you
call lots
of lizards?

A **FLAMBOYANCE** of **F**

A PARTY of

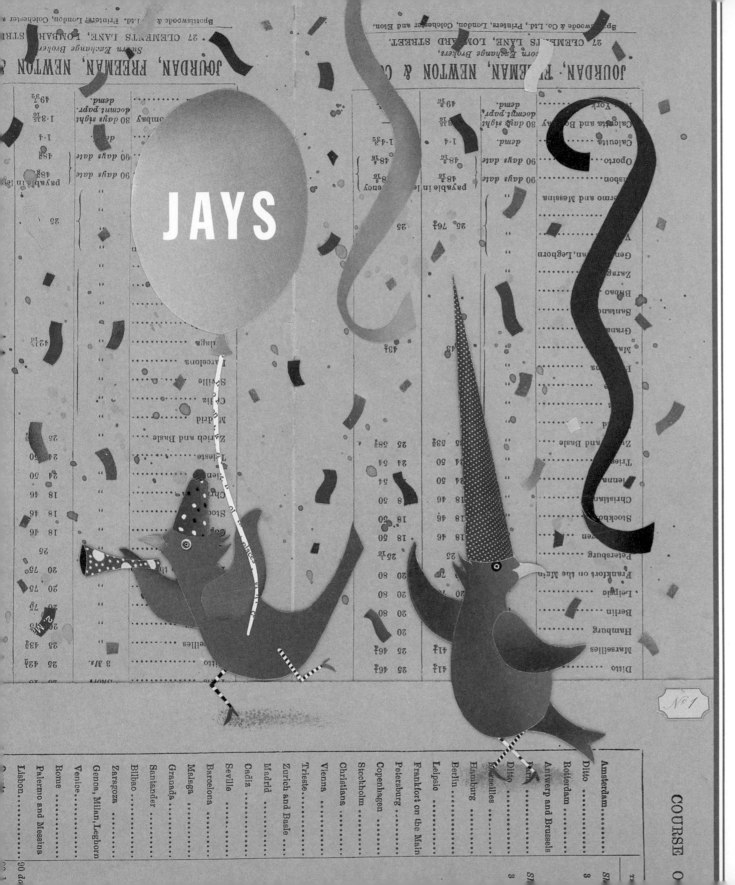

JAYS

More than one jay is called a **PARTY** of jays.

It sure is! How about an assembly of all different animals? What do you call that?

Collective nouns are names for groups of people, animals, or objects: words such as flock, herd, assembly, and array.

Many originated in medieval England and were published in courtesy books, etiquette guides for young aristocrats.

Some of the collective nouns in this book first appeared in *The Book of St. Albans*, in a section on hunting attributed to a woman named "Dam[e] Julyans Barnes" and printed in England in 1486. It was one of the earliest books to record collective nouns.

Many of the animals listed in *The Book of St. Albans* were "beasts of the chase," but also included were group names for all sorts of animals and birds. These collective nouns were often playful or poetic references to the animal's behavior, characteristics, or appearance.

"A mischief of mice" and "a memory of elephants" are two collective nouns that have no clear lineage. Nevertheless we were so smitten with them that we included them in this menagerie!

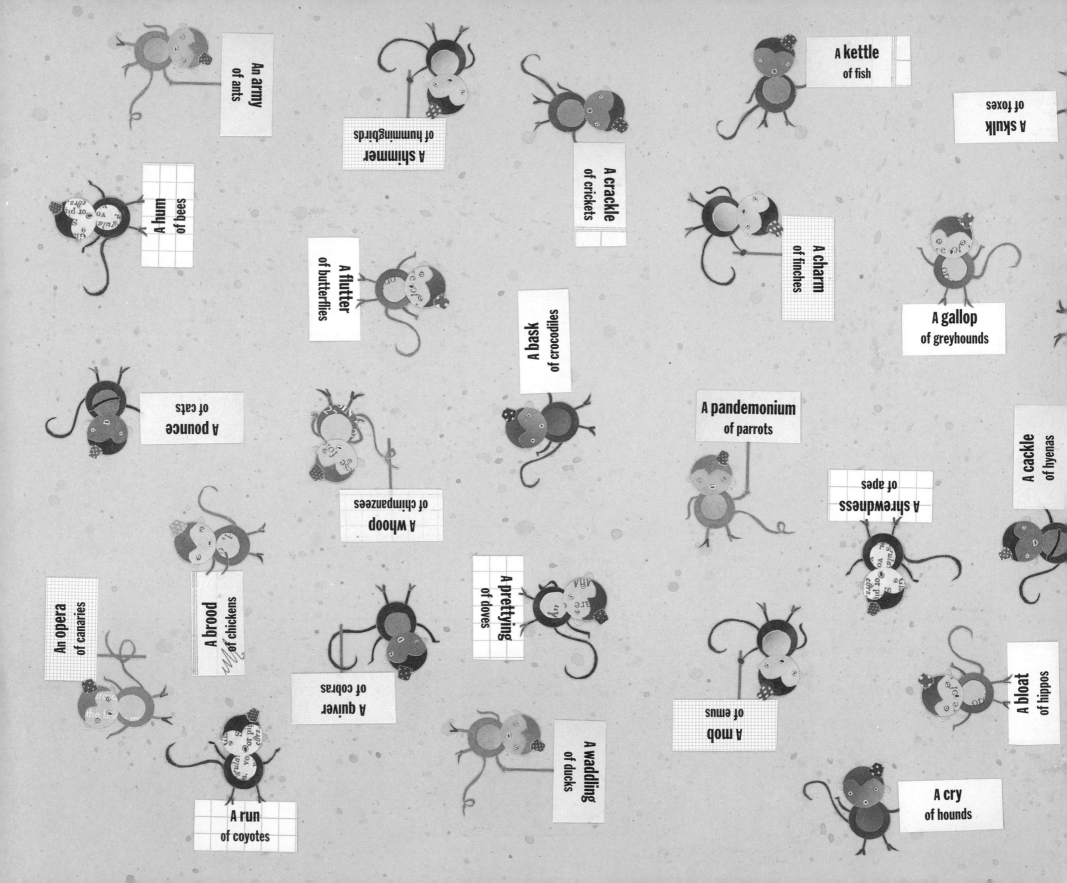